The Harp Mouse Chooses Her Home: The Adventure Begins

By
Diane E. Dunn

Illustrated by
Donna Pellegata

**Dedicated to my brother, David,
who has always loved music and mice**

A Special Thank You To:

Denise Grupp-Verbon,
Toledo, Ohio

Timothy Habinski of Timothy Harps,
Forest, Ontario, Canada

Visit us on the web at
www.heartandharp.net

ISBN 13: 978-0-9742174-1-3

Published by Heart & Harp, L.L.C.
P.O. Box 818
Walled Lake, MI 48390

Layout and design by Josh Visser

Printed in U.S.A.

The little brown field mouse stood up on her hind legs. She balanced on a nearby twig to get a better look at the warm and cozy cabin at the edge of the trees. She had been near the cabin before, but feeling the chill in the air today, she wanted to go inside the cabin and look around.

She ran though the long grass and came to the door of the cabin. The front door was open, so she looked around quickly and then scampered in.

Once inside the cabin, she saw that it was not a house, but a workshop. It smelled of fresh wood, sawdust, and other good things. As she looked around, the little mouse saw wood shavings and tools. On the workbench was something that was made of dark new wood. She was curious to see what it was.

Before she could crawl up onto the workbench to see the wooden object, she heard a noise at the door. She darted into a corner and hid behind a barrel.

Someone was coming through the front door. From her hiding place the little mouse peeked out to see who it was. A man came into the workshop, went to the workbench, and picked up the wooden object.

As the man picked up the object made of wood, the little brown mouse could see that it was quite large and was shaped like a triangle.

The mouse watched as the man began to put strings into the wood. For each string he tied a knot inside the wood, then pulled the string through and fastened it on top of the triangle.

As she crept closer, the mouse saw that the strings were different colors. After the man put many strings through the wood, he tightened them and ran a finger across them. A sound came from those strings!

The mouse saw the man begin to smile. He used a tool to tighten each string. He plucked each string with his finger, and the strings sounded even more beautiful!

The mouse watched in amazement as the man took the wooden object with the colored strings down from the workbench and put it on the floor.

He pulled up a stool, sat down behind the wooden object, put his fingers on the strings, and said, "A harp is not a harp until it has been played."

As the man began plucking the strings, the mouse heard the most beautiful sounds she had ever heard. She listened as the man played many different melodies.

After the man had played for a long time, he smiled, got up, and left the workshop. The mouse inched closer to the wooden object so she could see it better. She had heard the man call it a harp, so now she knew its name.

Because the harp had been placed on the floor, the mouse was now able to see that there were large holes in the back of the harp.

A few minutes later the man came back with a large padded cover. His wife was with him, and as they came through the door, he said, "This harp is finished, so I can send it to its new owner." His wife nodded, smiled, and together they began to put the padded cover on the harp.

The little brown mouse knew that she wanted to go wherever that beautiful harp was going. She did not know where it was being sent, but she knew that she wanted to go with it.

The harpmaker and his wife had not finished putting the cover on the harp. The little brown mouse waited for the right moment when the man and woman were not looking. The mouse scampered across the workshop floor, ran up to the harp, and crawled inside.

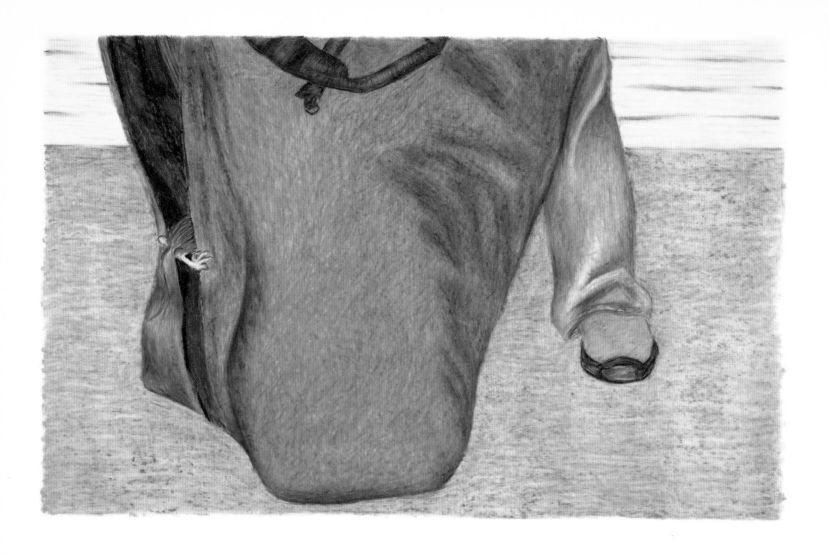

And so the little brown field mouse became a harp mouse. She was about to begin her wonderful adventures.

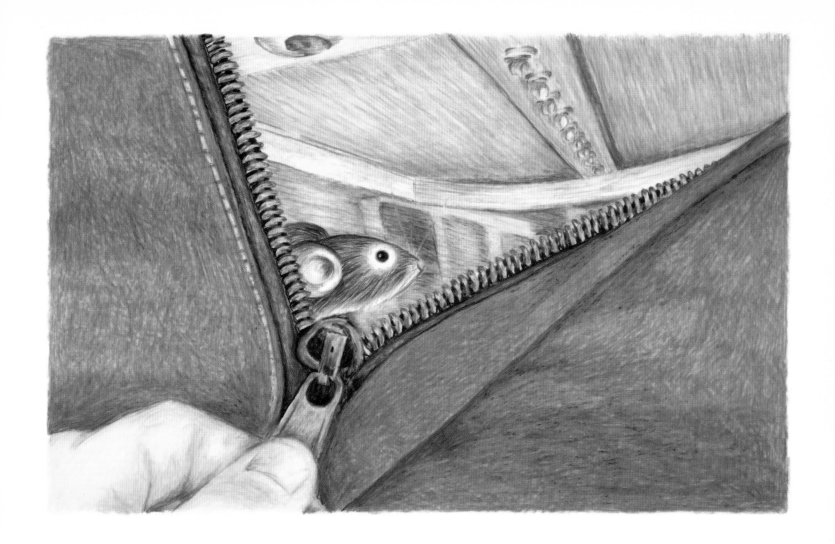

The little brown mouse felt cozy and warm in the darkness as the harpmaker and his wife finished covering the harp.

The mouse shifted her position in the base of the harp as the harp was gently laid on its side. She felt at home with all the good smells of fresh wood inside the harp. Although she could not see them, she also knew the beautiful colored strings that made the music were just above the place where she was resting.

The little brown field mouse curled up in the darkness at the bottom of the harp. She was so excited to see where she would be when the cover was taken off the harp.

As she drifted into sleep, she dreamed of her future and knew it would be full of wonderful adventures and beautiful music.